A MUCH Later Meeting

By Zoe Burton

A MUCH Later Meeting

Zoe Burton

Published by Zoe Burton

Early drafts of this story were written and posted on fan fiction forums in July 2020.

ISBN-13: 978-1953138033

Acknowledgements

First, I thank Jesus Christ, my Savior and Guide, without whom this story would not have been told. Thank you, and I love you!

As always, I thank my friends, Rose and Leenie. I love you, too! <3

Finally, thank you to my sixteen Patrons at Patreon, whose unflagging support means more than I can say. <3

Table of Contents

Chapter 1

Longbourn, Hertfordshire

1840

Elizabeth Bennet leaned toward the mirror and added a last touch of balm to her lips. Rolling them together, she leaned back again and examined her reflection.

Time had treated Elizabeth well. Her chestnut curls only had a few streaks of silver in them. There were some creases around her eyes, but her cheeks were as smooth as ever. Her figure had matured a bit, but she still walked every day and so had not run to fat. She stood to examine the fit of her gown.

Fashion had changed quite a bit since Elizabeth's come-out more than thirty years ago. Waistlines had fallen from just under the bust to the natural waist, which meant longer corsets. Elizabeth hated them. She hated being constricted so much. However, if she wished to look her best, not to mention keep from causing a scandal, she must wear the devilish devices.

Skirts had transformed, too, from long, straight lines to bell shapes. Elizabeth turned to the tall, free-standing mirror to the left of her dressing table. She tilted her head as she looked critically at her reflection. While she disliked the style, she did look well in it. A knock on the door of her bedchamber brought her out of her reverie.

"Yes?"

"The carriage is ready, ma'am. Mr. Dalrymple is waiting in the drawing room." The housekeeper,

Mrs. Cowher, called through the door.

Elizabeth strode to the portal and opened it. "Tell my nephew I will be down directly." She smiled at the servant, who curtseyed and hastened back down the hallway.

Elizabeth looked around the room. Seeing her reticule and shawl laid out on the end of the bed, she picked them up, draping the latter over her arm and looping the former over the wrist of the same hand. Then, she stepped into the hall and pulled the door closed behind her.

Elizabeth gracefully made her way down the stairs. Reaching the ground floor of the house, she turned left and entered the door to her father's book room. Mr. Bennet, now eighty years of age, was too frail to walk up and down the steps. He lived in this room, by his own preference. Elizabeth often tried to entice him to spend time with her elsewhere in the house, but he refused.

"Ah, Elizabeth. Come to see your old Papa before you go to the ball?" Bennet's eyes gleamed at the sight of his only unmarried daughter. He lifted his cheek for her to kiss.

"I am." Elizabeth obliged him before glancing around the room, then at the desk behind which her father sat. "Did you eat? Is there anything I can get you before I leave?"

"I did. Finished the entire plate, too. You can ask Mrs. Cowher if you don't believe me." Bennet nodded once and grinned. "I heard voices a bit ago."

"Yes, Mary sent Neville to escort me to the assembly. I told her I was plenty old enough to not need a chaperone, but you know Mary." Elizabeth winked at her father.

Bennet chuckled. "Indeed." He patted Elizabeth's hand where it rested on his shoulder. "I am happy she did. Even a nephew is better than no escort at all. You enjoy yourself tonight. Do not sit there worrying about me. I have the Cowhers if I need anything."

"Promise me you will not give that sweet woman a hard time."

With a wink and a grin, Bennet replied. "Would I do that?" When Elizabeth rolled her eyes, he patted her hand again. "I will do my best. Go, now, and tell young Neville I expect him to pay his respects when he drops you off in the morning."

"I will." Elizabeth kissed Bennet's cheek again, then took a moment to straighten the blanket over his shoulders. "I will see you later. I

11

love you." With another sweeping, sharp-eyed glance over the contents of the room, she walked to the door and out, closing it behind her.

Neville must have heard the book room door shut, because Elizabeth was only halfway across the entry hall when he popped his head out of the drawing room. "There you are, Aunt Lizzy. Is Grandpapa well?"

Elizabeth accepted a kiss to the cheek from her sister's youngest child. "He is. He said to tell you he expects a visit when you drop me off after the ball."

"I knew I could not sneak in here and back out without him noticing. Sharp as a tack he is, despite his age. He likely intends to demand the shilling I owe him."

"You and your grandfather are gambling again?" Elizabeth's left brow rose.

Neville blushed. "He bet me I couldn't recite a section of Virgil's Aeneid in Latin. I couldn't."

Elizabeth grinned and rolled her eyes. "I am surprised you allowed him to goad you into that."

With a sheepish grin and a laugh, Neville agreed. He took Elizabeth's shawl and draped it over her shoulders. "Shall we go? Mama will wonder what is taking so long."

~~~***~~~

A half hour later, Elizabeth sat in the Meryton Assembly Room beside her next youngest sister.

"How is Papa tonight?" Mary smiled at her husband, David, who had just handed her and Elizabeth each a cup of punch.

"He is well. He seemed happier tonight than he has been for a while now. It appears he persuaded your son to place a bet. Neville lost." Elizabeth smirked.

Mary rolled her eyes at her father's antics. "He is a bad influence, but how can anyone tell him no?" She shook her head. "Does he still mention Mama?"

"Every now and then, yes." Elizabeth took a sip of her punch. "Usually around the time of her birthday or their wedding anniversary. I am still uncertain he really loved her, but he does become nostalgic."

Just then, the attention of the ladies was taken by the entrance of a group of strangers into the room.

Mary leaned over and whispered in her sister's ear. "Those are Neville's friends, and the uncle of one."

Elizabeth lifted her chin in acknowledgement of her sister's information as she gazed at the group of gentlemen who were being greeted by John Lucas. "Have you met any?"

"Yes, the tall gentleman with blond hair. His name is Lord Bertram Frary, Viscount Hucknall. I believe the older one behind him, with the dark hair, is his uncle, though I do not know his name."

Elizabeth nodded again, her gaze riveted to the tall, distinguished, older gentleman as he trailed the group of younger men through the room. Suddenly, he turned his head and their eyes met and held. Riveted in place, she nearly forgot to curtsey as he walked past, until Mary tugged at her hand. Elizabeth dipped, dropping her eyes and blushing. When she rose and looked up, the gentleman was still looking at her, but he quickly snapped his head forward again. She stared after him, her heart pounding.

Elizabeth and Mary spent the next quarter hour circulating amongst their neighbors and friends, making small talk and catching up on local gossip. Mary's husband came to claim her for a dance, and Neville requested Elizabeth's company for the same set.

A little while later, Elizabeth was sitting out a set on the opposite side of the room. The dark haired gentleman she had admired was standing a few feet away, staring out at the dance floor. Before long, the young blond man who was Neville's friend approached the gentleman and spoke to him.

At the same time, Neville walked up to his aunt, taking her

hand and making her laugh. He kissed her fingers as she shooed him away. "Go tease your mother, you young scamp."

As Neville strode back across the room, Elizabeth heard his friend and uncle speak.

"Come, Uncle Darcy, you must dance. I hate to see you standing about like this."

"You know I dislike dancing unless I am particularly known to my partner. Dancing with strangers is insupportable." Darcy's deep voice was tinged with annoyance.

"Mama warned me you would say that. She said it is no wonder you never married, since you refuse to speak to anyone to whom you are not already intimately acquainted." Lord Hucknall looked over his uncle's shoulder. "Look, over there. She likes to dance, as I understand

17

it. She is Dalrymple's aunt; I will ask him to introduce us."

Darcy turned and looked at Elizabeth. He examined her from head to toe, finally catching her eye. "I learned a long time ago not to give insult by refusing to dance with a lady when prompted, if she was close enough to hear my conversation. If you will procure an introduction, I will ask her to dance the next set."

"Excellent!" Lord Hucknall grinned. "Stay there; I will return shortly."

True to his word, Darcy's nephew approached not five minutes later, his friend in tow.

"Frary tells me you would like an introduction to my aunt."

"I would, if you would oblige me."

After a long pause, while Neville stared at Darcy, appearing to take his measure, the young gentleman agreed. "Very well. Come with me." He moved past the older man and approached his aunt, who had been engaged in conversation with an elderly widow in the seat beside her. "Aunt Lizzy, I apologize for interrupting."

With a smile, Elizabeth excused herself from her neighbor and gave her attention to her nephew. "You may interrupt me anytime, as you well know. What can I do for you?"

"There is someone who would like to meet you." Neville gestured to Darcy.

"Oh." Elizabeth stood, clasping her hands in front of her. "Please do introduce us."

Neville smiled and turned to Darcy and Hucknall. "This blond fellow here is a friend from school. Mama has met him already and given him her seal of approval." Neville winked at his aunt. "This is Lord Bertram Frary, Viscount Hucknall. Frary, this is my aunt, Miss Elizabeth Bennet." Neville then gestured to Darcy. "This is Frary's uncle on his mother's side, Mr. Fitzwilliam Darcy of Pemberley in Derbyshire and Darcy House in London. Mr. Darcy, this is my aunt, Miss Elizabeth Bennet."

Hucknall and Darcy both bowed to Elizabeth's curtsey.

"I am pleased to make your acquaintance." Elizabeth's ever-present smile hid the sudden bout of nerves that hit her at learning the name of the man she had admired from afar.

The orchestra resumed playing, and Neville and the viscount started.

"I have to find my partner." Neville leaned over and kissed his aunt's cheek, then he and his friend scurried off to dance.

Darcy watched them go with a half-smile lifting the corner of his lips. He turned to Elizabeth. "Miss Bennet, may I have this dance?" He held up a hand, palm out. "I warn you I am a bit out of practice. I cannot vouch for the safety of your dancing slippers."

Elizabeth chuckled. "You may have this dance, sir. I will endeavor to keep my dancing slippers out of your path." She slipped her hand into the crook of the elbow Darcy extended out to her.

Chapter 2

Thankfully for the couple, the first dance of the set was a waltz, which would enable them to converse. Darcy stepped in time with the first notes of music, whirling Elizabeth around. He searched his mind for something to say. Holding this woman in his arms, feeling her waist under his hand and smelling her perfume, had scrambled his thoughts. He felt like a besotted young man instead of the wise elder gentleman that he was. He knew conversation was important to ladies, however, and so said the first thing that came to his mind. "You are young Dalrymple's aunt?"

"I am." Elizabeth's eyes twinkled. "His favorite, I do believe."

Darcy's lips twitched. "Indeed? What evidence do you have to prove your case?"

A smile threatened to overtake Elizabeth. Her lips twitched as she held it at bay. "He visits me most often of all."

Darcy shook his head. "According to my nephew, you are the only aunt of Dalrymple's that lives in the area." Darcy waited with bated breath to see what Elizabeth would say.

Elizabeth's grin finally broke free. "It is hardly my fault the rest of my sisters live so far away. 'Tis their loss, do you not think?"

Darcy laughed out loud at Elizabeth's impertinent response. "I would have to agree." A tender feeling filled his chest when her warm gurgle of laughter joined his. "Tell me, Miss Bennet, how it is that a lovely lady such as yourself remains unmarried." He tilted his head and examined her face and hair. "If I had my guess, you are of an age with Dalrymple's parents."

"Yes, his mother is my next youngest sister. I have remained unmarried because I never found anyone I could respect or esteem enough to tie myself to for the entirety of my life. Instead, I have devoted my adult years to teaching my sisters' children to play the pianoforte incredibly ill and to sketch the characters of all they meet." Elizabeth smirked when Darcy laughed again. "And you, Mr. Darcy? Is there a Mrs. Darcy?"

Darcy shook his head. "No, there is not. Like you, I have never found anyone who I thought I could make my partner in life. Lord Hucknall is my heir. He is my only sister's eldest son." He paused and then, not knowing why he was confessing this to a total stranger but unable to stop his tongue, continued, "I felt at a young age there was a lady specifically set aside for me. I used to dream about her, vivid dreams of a life shared with love and laughter." He shrugged and blushed. "I never met anyone who made me feel as my dream lady did, so I remain alone."

Elizabeth smiled softly. "I understand. I also had dreams long ago, only of a young man. My friend Charlotte used to tell me there is always hope. Of course, she married the ridiculous man who was to be heir of my father's estate when she was seven and twenty, because she felt she was a burden to her parents."

"Ah, yes. She would hardly be a good source of information on the topic, then."

26

Elizabeth laughed again. "Exactly."

"Do you live with your sister?"

"No, I live on my father's estate. He recently turned eighty and has become rather frail. My mother has been gone for several years, so it is only me and Papa at home now."

"I am sorry for your loss. My mother died when my sister was a baby and my father when I was barely out of University. The pain of losing a parent never dissipates. It merely fades."

"Yes. I was not Mama's favorite child, but I loved her fiercely, as I do all my family."

By now, the waltz was ending. The next dance of the set was to be a country dance, but it was slow enough that Darcy and Elizabeth could continue their conversation.

Zoe Burton

"Do you have brothers?" The longer Darcy spoke to Elizabeth, the more he wanted to know.

"I do not. I have four sisters." Elizabeth lifted her chin, a mischievous look on her face.

Darcy's brows rose. "Four sisters? Your poor father!" He grinned at Elizabeth's laugh. "Where do you fall in amongst them?"

"I am the second. My eldest sister is Jane. She is married to an associate of our uncle's and lives in London." Elizabeth tilted her head. "You may have heard of my brother-in-law. Jane says he is in high demand amongst the male members of the *ton*. He makes custom knives and fencing foils. His specialty is canes with blades inside the tips."

Darcy's eyes widened. "Beauclerk?"

Elizabeth grinned. "The very one. Cornwallis Beauclerk. He recently purchased an estate a few miles away, so his family has somewhere to go in the summer, but he prefers to remain close to his business most of the year, which means London. It will be nice to have my sister near enough for frequent visits again."

Darcy whistled. "You have some valuable connections, Miss Bennet."

Elizabeth shook her head, ignoring his statement. "I told you already that Neville's mother is my next youngest sister. The one after her we call Kitty. She married a clergyman and lives in Essex. My youngest sister eloped with a soldier in the militia within days of Jane's wedding and now lives in New Castle. Her husband joined the regular army after their marriage and was sent to the continent when Napoleon was still creating havoc. He became a hero and was promoted to the rank of colonel."

"So you are scattered all over the country." Darcy took Elizabeth's hands and skipped down the line with her, as the dance steps dictated.

"We are. We write letters as often as we can, and visit whenever possible. The train makes that feasible even for Lydia and her brood. When I was a girl, it would have taken a week to get to New Castle. Now it takes only a few hours."

Darcy snorted. "I vividly recall those days. Do you have many nieces and nephews?"

"I have sixteen in total, not including grand nephews and nieces." Elizabeth proudly lifted her chin. "Each of my sisters has a fine family, and Jane and Mary have grandchildren already."

Darcy smiled. "My sister has three children, the viscount, a younger son, and a girl."

Elizabeth tilted her head. "You have no brothers?"

"I am afraid not. I have only one sibling, and that is Georgiana. She is more than ten years my junior."

"She is a countess?"

Darcy nodded. "Yes. Her first season, she fell in love with Lord Lucas Frary, who was then Viscount Hucknall. His father died when Bertram was an infant. His seat is Ashfield."

"Earl Ashfield ... I have read of him in the papers. He has done much good for the country."

"Yes, he is a very good sort of fellow. I grilled him when he came to ask for Georgiana's hand, but he stood up to every test I put him through. He has been an excellent husband to my sister."

"If your father died when you were just coming of age and your mother was gone when your sister was a baby, you must have raised her."

"I did. I made many mistakes, but in the end, she became a lovely and accomplished young lady with a heart of gold. She is very happy and it delights me to see my shy little sister become a leader in the *ton*." Darcy lifted his chin, his eyes shining with pride.

Elizabeth smiled. "I am certain she is every bit as proud of you as you are of her."

The last notes of the music faded away and Darcy and Elizabeth stood across from each other, their gazes locked. He bowed and she curtseyed, then he approached. "May I call on you tomorrow? My nephew has rented a nearby estate, Netherfield. I understand it is not far from Meryton?"

"It is not." Elizabeth's smile grew wide. "Netherfield is the estate closest to Longbourn. I would be delighted if you called on me."

Darcy's grin lighted his face. He held out his elbow to her. "Thank you. I look forward to tomorrow. In the meantime, perhaps we could get some refreshments together."

Elizabeth tucked her hand in his elbow once more. "I would like that, very much."

Early the next morning, after Neville had returned Elizabeth to Longbourn and she had checked on her father, she left Bennet and his grandson in the book room and ascended the stairs to her bed chamber. Her maid, Hannah, was waiting for her and soon Elizabeth was in bed, her hair brushed and braided and her ball gown and underthings exchanged for a night shift. She blew out the candle by her bed and settled down under the covers, her mind filled with Fitzwilliam Darcy.

Elizabeth recalled every feature of his face, from the dark eyes and noble mien to the grey at his temples. His hair and body are that of a young man, still, she thought. Other than the lighter color at the temples, his hair is a rich black. And his form! So strong. His arm was quite muscular under my fingers. He was graceful, as well. She sighed and turned over. I have not been this excited about a gentleman in decades. I shall have to write Jane about him on the morrow.

Soon, Elizabeth was asleep, and for the first time in many years, she had a recurrence of a specific dream she had experienced frequently in her youth; a dream of a handsome young man and a tender kiss.

Chapter 3

Darcy woke, as was his wont, shortly after dawn. He stretched, then lay on his back with his fingers laced and his hands under his head. His mind was filled with the remnants of a dream he had not had in years. He grinned. His thoughts wandered to Miss Elizabeth Bennet. "She looks so much like the woman in my dream," he murmured to himself. He recalled their dances and conversation, reliving every moment and marveling at the feelings of comfort and belonging that filled him in her presence. Finally, hearing his valet moving about in the dressing room, he sighed and rose to begin his day.

A short while later, Darcy wandered down the stairs to the

breakfast room, intent on having a cup of coffee and a pastry before going for a ride. He had just settled into a chair at the table when Viscount Hucknall strolled in, dressed in his riding clothes.

"Good morning, Uncle. Did you sleep well?"

Darcy smiled. "I did. The bed was comfortable and I was very tired."

Hucknall grinned over his shoulder. He began to speak as he looked back at the sideboard, selecting eggs, kippers, and toast for his plate. "The beds here are very nice." He turned around, allowing his gaze to wander over the space, and then approached the table. Setting his plate next to Darcy's, he sat, nodding to the footman who offered him coffee.

Darcy shook his head as he watched his nephew make short

work of the pile of food. "I see you still have a hollow leg." His eyes twinkled as he lifted his cup and sipped.

The viscount smirked. "So it seems." He shrugged. "The amount of food served last night was small and inadequate. I suppose I could have sent down for some meat and cheese when we arrived home last night, but I did not wish to put the cook to any trouble."

"That was thoughtful of you." Darcy rose to return to the sideboard and choose something else to eat. "Your mother would be proud of you."

Hucknall winked at Darcy. "Be sure to tell her, will you? She needs to hear from more than me that I am well behaved."

Darcy rolled his eyes. "Scamp," he muttered, just loud

enough for his nephew to hear. With his plate now full of ham and eggs, he turned back and resumed his place. "I thought to go riding after breakfast. Care to join me?"

Hucknall swallowed down the last of his meal. "I would. Have you plans for the afternoon?" He pushed back his plate and sipped his coffee, his eyes on his uncle.

"As a matter of fact, I do." Darcy stabbed a piece of ham with his fork and lifted it. "I intend to visit Longbourn today." He stuffed the meat in his mouth and chewed, watching his nephew's brows lift.

"Longbourn?"

Darcy nodded. "Yes, Longbourn. Your friend's aunt lives there."

The viscount lowered his cup, his eyes glued to Darcy's face.

"You are calling on Dalrymple's aunt?" He whistled. "You have never called on a woman before."

Darcy shrugged, his mouth full of food. He finished chewing, swallowed, and wiped his lips. "I have never met a lady as fascinating as Miss Bennet before."

Hucknall stared at Darcy. He slowly nodded. "Yes, I can see that. Shall I write to Mama about it, or would you rather I wait?"

"How about you not mention it at all, ever?" Darcy frowned and pointed his fork at his nephew. "It is none of my sister's business, and if there is news, I will tell her."

The viscount lifted his hands and leaned back. "Very well. I will keep it to myself. You can put away that Darcy glare."

Darcy glowered at his nephew a little longer, just to make his point clear. Then, stabbing the remainder of his meal, he quickly ate it and washed it down with coffee. He stood. "Are you ready yet?"

~~~***~~~

That afternoon, Darcy's carriage entered the paddock at Longbourn. He twisted his neck, his cravat suddenly constricting his ability to breathe. He clenched his sweaty, glove-covered palms, wishing he could wipe the moisture on his breeches. When the equipage came to a stop, he waited for the groom to open the door and kick down the step. His heart pounding, he took a deep breath and descended, looking up at the well-kept home that was about the size of Netherfield. He tugged on his waistcoat and strode up the steps.

The door opened at his knock. A woman in the dress of a housekeeper accepted his card.

"I am here to see Miss Bennet."

"Of course, sir. She is in the drawing room, if you will follow me."

Darcy did as the woman bid, pausing outside the door as she announced him, and then striding into the room. What he saw made his breath catch in his throat.

Elizabeth rose from a sofa in the center of the room, a smile brightening her countenance. The blue dress she was wearing complemented her dark hair. Though she was covered from her neck to her toes, the wide skirt and shoulders and cinched-in waist showed off her womanly curves to perfection. She curtseyed, and it was this action that snapped Darcy out of his silent admiration.

"Good afternoon, Mr. Darcy. I am so pleased you called." Elizabeth gestured to the other end of her sofa. "Please, do be seated. Would you care for some tea?" When Darcy indicated he would enjoy a cup, she turned to Mrs. Cowher. "Bring the tea tray in, and some of those crumpets Cook made this morning."

When the housekeeper had curtseyed and made her exit, Elizabeth sat, Darcy joining her.

"You look very well today, Miss Bennet." Darcy cringed inwardly at the inane comment.

"Thank you. You look well, also. Very dashing." Elizabeth grinned.

Darcy could not help the chuckle that rumbled through him. "Thank you." He glanced around the large but comfortable room. "You have a lovely place in which to entertain."

"I do; I thank you." Elizabeth looked around. "I suppose it is a bit outdated. My mother redecorated shortly before my elder sister married, and it has not been touched since. It is familiar, however, and as I am not overly interested in refurbishing, it remains." She laughed. "As long as the paper is not peeling off the walls, I am not going to worry."

Darcy grinned. "I do not blame you for avoiding it." He shuddered. "I allowed my sister to redecorate my townhouse in London a few years ago and it was a mess. I should hate to live through that again."

"Exactly!" Elizabeth giggled. "We are of the same mind on the issue, it seems."

"Indeed, we are." Darcy paused. "Perhaps there are other things we have in common. Do you like to read?"

"I do!" Elizabeth leaned forward. "I read everything I can get my hands on." She waved her hand in the direction of the door. "I have gone through every book in my father's study more than once, and have a subscription at the lending library, as well."

Darcy was riveted by the animation on Elizabeth's face. "My favorite way to pass time is to read. Do you favor one kind of book over the others? I prefer histories, myself."

Elizabeth's eyes twinkled. "I thought you might." She tilted her head for a moment as she looked at Darcy, but then straightened it and replied to his query. "I love history, but I find I prefer plays, particularly Shakespeare's comedies. I love a laugh, and what better way to find one than to read one?"

"I am not at all surprised. You are uniformly cheerful, from what I have learned of you so far." Darcy chuckled when Elizabeth blushed.

The conversation turned to music while they had their tea, and by the time they were finished, it was past time for Darcy to take his leave.

"Would you care for a walk in the gardens before I go?" Darcy held his breath as he waited for Elizabeth's reply.

"I would love one. Do you mind if I check on my father before we do?"

"Not at all. I will come with you, if you do not object. I should greatly enjoy meeting the gentleman who raised such a charming daughter." Darcy stood and extended his arm.

Elizabeth placed her hand in Darcy's and allowed him to help her up. She smiled at him as she teased him. "Those are very pretty words, Mr. Darcy. One might think you were trying to charm me."

Darcy smiled. "Perhaps I am." He tucked Elizabeth's hand into the crook of his elbow. "Lead the way, madam."

With a grin, Elizabeth began walking, leading Darcy across the entry hall and just past the staircase. She knocked on a closed door and waited. "Papa?"

"Enter."

Darcy could barely hear the response from inside the room, but Elizabeth clearly did, immediately pressing the latch and pushing the door open.

"Papa, I have someone I wish you to meet." Elizabeth looked over her shoulder and gestured to Darcy to enter behind her. When he was standing at her side, she looked at Bennet. "Papa, this is Mr. Darcy. He expressed a desire to be introduced to you. I met him at the assembly last night."

Bennet lowered the book in his hand to the desk in front of him. "Did he now? Well, bring him in. Is this the gentleman young Neville was telling me about? The stranger that danced with you?"

"He is, and I will have to speak to Neville about gossiping, for that is all it is when he speaks to you about my business, you know." Elizabeth led Darcy to stand before the desk.

"Will you take away all my fun, then?" Bennet clucked his tongue. "First you want me to stop teasing the housekeeper and now you accuse me of teaching my grandson to gossip. Soon there will be nothing left for me to entertain myself with." He laughed when Elizabeth's fists landed on her hips. "I will stop vexing you, for now." He winked, then turned his attention to his guest. "Forgive me for not standing, young man. At my age, I find I must limit the times I do, lest I become permanently bruised." He rubbed his arm. "The floor is quite hard."

Darcy bowed, his lips quirking up on one side. "Think nothing of it, sir."

"Papa, this is Mr. Fitzwilliam Darcy of Pemberley in Derbyshire." Elizabeth turned to Darcy. "Mr.

Darcy, this is my father, Mr. Thomas Bennet."

Bennet extended a hand to the younger man. "Welcome to Longbourn. I am pleased to meet you."

"Likewise. You have a lovely home." Darcy stepped forward and leaned over the desk to shake Bennet's hand.

"And a lovely daughter, as well, I suspect." Bennet chuckled when both Darcy and Elizabeth blushed.

"Papa!" Elizabeth rolled her eyes and shook her head. "Please forgive him, Mr. Darcy. He has become incorrigible in his dotage."

Darcy laughed. "I am not offended. I have every intention of being just as mischievous when I am his age."

Bennet joined in Darcy's laughter. "I like your young man,

Lizzy." He addressed Darcy. "Have you time to visit a while?"

"Unfortunately, I do not. I was just going to take a walk in the gardens with Miss Bennet before I leave." Darcy's words were tinged with regret.

"Consider yourself invited back to Longbourn. If Lizzy has no wish to see you, you can sit in here with me and discuss manly things instead of lace and finery." Bennet winked.

"Thank you. I look forward to the next time." Darcy grinned and bowed.

"Good, good." Bennet waved a hand toward the door. "Get on with you, then, and walk with my girl. She has not had a decent suitor in years. She needs the practice."

Elizabeth rolled her eyes again but said nothing. Instead, she straightened her father's bed, poured him a fresh glass of port, and wrapped an extra blanket around him. "I will be back shortly. I love you." She kissed his head before strolling around the desk and taking Darcy's offered arm. She smiled up at him. "Are you ready?"

Chapter 4

Darcy smirked and waved his hand toward the door. "Lead on."

Her mouth widening to a grin, Elizabeth did as she was bid, leading Darcy into the entry hall, then out the door and into the garden. They wandered around the paths for a quarter hour, before he reluctantly led them to his carriage.

"I really must go. I have intruded on your time for far too long today." Darcy faced Elizabeth, taking her hands in his. "I have very much enjoyed this visit."

Elizabeth's lips lifted as she rushed to reassure her guest. "I have had a wonderful time with you today. It has been no intrusion, I assure you."

Darcy seemed to relax a little. "Good. May I call on you again?"

"You may. When?" Elizabeth's small smile grew.

Darcy chuckled. "Tomorrow?"

Elizabeth's growing smile widened again and she beamed at him. "Excellent! I will be here waiting for you."

Darcy said nothing, his smile almost as large as his companion's. He allowed his gaze to roam her features before settling on her sparkling eyes. Finally, he lifted both of her hands and kissed them. With a light squeeze, he let them go, turning and ascending into the waiting carriage.

Elizabeth waved as the large equipage began to move. She watched it pull out of the paddock, finally turning to go into the house when it reached the end of the drive and turned onto the roadway.

~~~***~~~

Darcy returned, as promised, the next day. The tea service had just been brought in when he and Elizabeth heard a knock on the door.

"I seem to be rather popular today." Elizabeth laughed. "The new Mrs. Goulding left just before you arrived, now you are here, and I have more visitors." She stood as the housekeeper opened the door, Darcy following suit.

"Mrs. Collins, ma'am."

"Charlotte! How lovely to see you! Come in, come in." Elizabeth looked past her friend to address Mrs. Cowher. "We will need additional hot water and tea items."

With a murmured, "Yes, ma'am," the housekeeper curtseyed and backed away, shutting the drawing room door behind her.

Zoe Burton

Elizabeth's attention returned to her oldest friend. "How are you, Charlotte, and your family?"

"We are well. Maria and her husband and girls returned to Bromley yesterday, and John and Edith have taken their youngest grandson back to Eton, so I am on my own for a few days. I thought I would make some visits to fill my time." Charlotte looked curiously at Darcy.

"I am happy you did." Elizabeth gestured to her other guest. "Did you meet Mr. Darcy at the assembly the other night? Mr. Darcy, this is my friend, Mrs. Collins. Charlotte, this is Mr. Darcy."

Darcy bowed. "I believe we were introduced, but you were called away before we had a chance to converse."

"Yes." Charlotte smiled. "My niece required my assistance."

58

Mrs. Cowher returned just then with the required tea items, catching Elizabeth's attention.

"Shall we sit?" Elizabeth and Darcy resumed their places on the settee, with Charlotte taking a chair nearer to Darcy's end than her friend's. Elizabeth busied herself with pouring the tea, leaving her guests to fill in the conversational gap.

Charlotte Collins had been a widow for several years. Her late husband had been a rector and the heir to Longbourn. He had not been a poorly-favored gentleman, but his ridiculous, obsequious, and conceited behavior had overshadowed the good in him, both in looks and personality. He had left her with little, just her small dowry and an insignificant savings; no home or assurance of additional income.

Now here Charlotte sat in the same room with Mr. Darcy of Derbyshire, who she knew from her brother was not only single, but wealthy. I married without love before, surely I can do it again, she thought. Silently deciding to woo him towards her, Charlotte began to question him. "How do you like it here in Hertfordshire, Mr. Darcy?"

"I find it very beautiful." Darcy's gaze darted to Elizabeth briefly. "It is not as wild and untamed as the Peaks, where my estate is located, but it has a gentleness to it that draws me."

Elizabeth handed a cup of tea to Darcy and another to Charlotte. She poured her own, then watched as her old friend and her new one spoke. Blowing on the tea in her cup, she sipped, looking at the other woman and wondering at her behavior. She tilted her head. If I did not know any better, I would say Charlotte is flirting with Mr. Darcy, she thought. But, that is not possible. Charlotte has said for years she had no intentions of marrying again. With a slight crease between her brows, she listened as Darcy described his estate. She noticed that his gaze frequently landed on her and lingered. I hope he likes me. I certainly do him.

"Have either of you ever visited the Peaks?" Darcy was eager to include Elizabeth in the conversation.

"I was there once, long ago, with my Aunt and Uncle Gardiner. It was breathtaking." Elizabeth set her cup on the tray in front of her. "We spent a fortnight seeing all that we could see. It was wonderful, and remains a favorite memory."

"I am happy to hear you were pleased with it." Darcy grinned at Elizabeth before turning to Charlotte. "And you, Mrs. Collins?"

"I am afraid I have never been. My husband was not a great traveler and our funds did not stretch beyond coming home here to Meryton once or twice a year."

"I am sorry to hear it. Maybe someday you will be able to make the trip." Darcy tilted his head. "You said your husband *was* not a great traveler?"

"Yes, I did. My husband passed away more than a decade ago. Closer to two, actually." Charlotte drained her cup and passed it back to Elizabeth. "He was the rector of a parish in Kent. There was a sickness that went through and while he was ministering to the ill, he caught it. His patroness' daughter also caught it and died."

"I am sorry for your loss." Darcy's brow creased. "My cousin lived in Kent and died when an illness swept through. My aunt also caught it; she recovered but was never the same and followed her daughter to the grave the following year. What parish did your husband have?"

"He had the Hunsford living. His patroness was Lady Catherine de Bourgh."

Darcy's brows shot up toward his hairline. "Indeed? Lady Catherine was my aunt. What a small world we live in!"

Charlotte's lips lifted in a slight smile. "It is small."

"I believe my Uncle de Bourgh's family inherited Rosings, since my cousin died before she married."

"Yes. He had come to visit your aunt not long after Miss de Bourgh's death. We were introduced, but I was in mourning and sorting through my husband's belongings, and so we were not afforded much conversation. Your aunt was very kind to allow me to stay on at Hunsford for a six-month while she searched for a new clergyman." Charlotte infused as much warmth into her tone as she could.

Darcy nodded. "I am not surprised to hear it. Though she enjoyed sticking her nose into the business of others far too much, she was known for her kindnesses, often in the most surprising of places. She had a superior air about her and a certainty that she was the most knowledgeable about everything under the sun. Her behavior put most people off, but she had a good heart."

Charlotte smiled broadly. "I found her just as you said. I will never forget what she did for me in my time of need."

Darcy's lips lifted in a small smile, but he said nothing else. Instead, he glanced at the clock on the mantel behind Elizabeth. "I have overstayed my welcome, I fear." He moved his gaze to his hostess. "I have greatly enjoyed our visit." He stood.

Elizabeth and Charlotte stood with him.

"I have, as well." Elizabeth's smile was not quite as bright as it normally was. She gripped her skirts and curtseyed.

"I should be going, too, Eliza. Do say you will come to Lucas

Lodge tomorrow for a chat." Charlotte took Elizabeth's hand.

"I will." Elizabeth's lips lifted briefly at the corners, but she looked more solemn than was her usual wont. Withdrawing her hand from her friend's, she clasped it with the other. "Shall I see you out?"

"That would be lovely." Darcy immediately offered Elizabeth an arm. His heart raced at her touch and he nearly forgot to offer the other to Charlotte. When she touched him, the experience was completely different to what it was when her friend did. Instead of a warm zing and a feeling of homecoming, he felt nothing. It was like having his sister hold his arm.

The trio walked to Longbourn's front door, where a maid waited with their hats, gloves, and outerwear. Darcy bowed to Elizabeth. "Thank you again. May I call tomorrow? I did not have the opportunity to visit with your father today."

Elizabeth's eyes never left Darcy's face. "You may. Shall I warn him you are coming?"

"If you wish." Darcy opened his mouth as though to say more but then glanced at Charlotte and closed it. He put his hat on his head and nodded. "Until tomorrow, Miss Bennet."

"Until tomorrow, Mr. Darcy." Elizabeth turned to her friend. "Thank you for coming, Charlotte. It was so good to see you." She hugged the other woman.

"You, as well." Charlotte glanced out the still-open door to see Darcy entering his carriage. "He is very nice."

"He is." Elizabeth's countenance became solemn. "I enjoy his company very much, as does my father."

Charlotte said nothing, instead smiling briefly. She put her bonnet on and tied the strings. "Do not forget to come visit. You can talk with me while Mr. Darcy speaks to Mr. Bennet."

Chapter 5

Elizabeth said nothing. She shut the door behind her friend and wondered what was going through Charlotte's mind. She wandered into her father's book room and sat in her favorite chair, beside his desk.

Bennet looked up from the tome he was peering at and laid his magnifying glass on the top of the desk, though he retained the book in his hand. "I heard voices. Did you have visitors?"

"I did. Charlotte and Mr. Darcy." Elizabeth looked down at her linked fingers.

"I see." Bennet chuckled, the sound more like a cackle than anything else. "Was Charlotte flirting with your suitor?"

Zoe Burton

Elizabeth rolled her eyes. "If I did not know better, I would think she was, but she has said since Mr. Collins passed on that she has no wish to marry again."

"She said that because there were no suitable candidates in Meryton." Bennet closed his book and pointed his finger at Elizabeth. "Your mother always said the Lucases were out for what they could get."

Elizabeth chuckled and looked at her hands. "She did." She was quiet for a moment. "If you think about it, when she accepted Collins, it was after she had invited him to Lucas Lodge after I refused him."

"I had forgotten about that, but it is true." Bennet tilted his head and examined his daughter. "What are you thinking? Surely you are not contemplating allow-

70

ing Charlotte Collins to take another suitor from you."

"She hardly took the first one, and you know it." Elizabeth frowned at her father for a moment, but then directed her gaze down again. "I have always behaved as a lady. I am not flirtatious like Lydia."

"Oh, you are most definitely flirtatious. What you are not is forward."

"Very well." Elizabeth inclined her head. "I am not forward, but I can be flirtatious. What I am trying to say is that I have never pushed myself forward to gain a gentleman's notice and I am not comfortable doing it now. If Mr. Darcy cannot see through Charlotte's machinations, is he really the gentleman I think he is?" She looked up, searching her father's countenance.

Bennet leaned back in his chair. "No, I daresay he is not, in that instance." He paused. "I have watched you for years, Elizabeth. You have gently rejected suitor after suitor, most having never gained permission for a visit following an introduction. You have long decried marriages that lack respect and esteem."

Elizabeth shrugged. "I have never found a gentleman who I felt either for to a large enough degree that I wished to spend my life with him."

"Exactly my point. Yet, I see you here today, at age ... what is it now .... fifty?" When Elizabeth nodded, Bennet continued. "Mr. Darcy brings a spring to your step that was not present before. I suspect you are half in love with him. Frankly, I believe he is the same with you. There was admiration in his every look when it was aimed at you. I do not wish to see you throw that away."

Elizabeth said nothing, simply staring at her father with a slightly stunned look. "You have never spoken of such things with me before. I do not know what to say."

Bennet shook his head. "Say nothing now, but think about it. You know how to demonstrate admiration without appearing wanton and loose. Pay attention to this man when you are in company together and see if what I am telling you is not true."

"I will. Thank you, Papa." Elizabeth reached her hand out across the top of her father's desk, gripping his when he placed it on top of her palm. "There. We have had one serious discussion today and that is our limit. Do you have your pocketwatch? What time is it now? Shall we have some tea brought in?"

Bennet squeezed Elizabeth's fingers, then let go. "Tea sounds lovely, my dear." He watched his daughter as she moved to the fireplace and pulled the cord that hung near it, then requested the beverage from the maid that answered the summons.

~~~***~~~

The next day, Darcy appeared at Longbourn early in the morning. Elizabeth was just returning from her morning walk when he rode up.

"Good morning, Miss Bennet," he called, doffing his hat.

"Good morning! What brings you to Longbourn so early?" Elizabeth stepped up onto the bottom of the staircase.

Darcy jumped off Apollo and tied the reins to the post beside the steps. "I remembered you were visiting Mrs. Collins today and wished to see you before you left."

Elizabeth blushed even as her eyes lit up at his words. Recalling what her father had suggested the afternoon before, she took a deep breath. "I am happy you did. Would you like to break your fast with us this morning? My father is up with the sun; he and I eat as many meals together as we can."

"If he would not mind the company, I would be delighted to." Darcy held his elbow out, grinning when the now-familiar frisson skated up his nerve endings to his heart.

Elizabeth's smirk matched her guest's as she tucked her hand in the crook of his elbow. "He will not mind at all."

75

~~~***~~~

Later that morning, Elizabeth left Bennet and Darcy in her father's book room, immersed in a game of chess. She walked to Lucas Lodge, with a wide smile that refused to diminish.

Charlotte greeted her oldest friend with a hug. "How are you?" She held Elizabeth's shoulders and leaned back. "You look radiant."

"I am very well, thank you for asking. I had a lovely walk and excellent company for breakfast."

Charlotte laughed. "You and your father have always been close. I think he has always preferred you even above the other gentlemen of the neighborhood."

Elizabeth shrugged, a smirk twisting one side of her lips up. "I do not know about that, but we certainly have always enjoyed each other's company." She followed her friend into the drawing room of Charlotte's home. Sinking gracefully to sit on a sofa next to the other woman, she asked, "How are you handling the solitude, with your brother and his family gone?"

Charlotte shrugged. "It is quiet, that is certain, but I find I bear it very well. I can pretend I am in my own home once more."

Elizabeth reached for her friend's hand. "You should form your own establishment. Surely there is someone with a small cottage you can rent nearby. Did I not hear recently that the dower house at the Great House at Stoke has become empty? There is that little house near Purvis Lodge, as well. Surely one of those would suit."

Charlotte smiled sadly. "No. My income would be sufficient for one, I am sure, but I would rather remain with my family."

"I understand. Truly, I do. It is only that it distresses me to see you relegated to the position of permanent guest."

Charlotte said nothing, instead pressing her lips together and changing the subject. "Did you hear the news about Viscount Hucknall?"

Elizabeth's brows drew together. She wished to pursue their original topic of conversation further, but seeing that her friend did not, allowed her attention to shift. "I have not. Is something the matter?"

"Oh, no." Charlotte reached out to lay a hand on Elizabeth's arm. "I apologize for frightening you. The viscount plans to hold a ball. His sister will come from London to be his hostess."

Elizabeth's brows had risen as she listened. "Neville did not say anything the last time I saw him. He must not have known."

"I heard it from Netherfield's steward. I saw him and his wife in Meryton yesterday afternoon." Charlotte began preparing the tea that had just been brought in by the maid. "Will you go?"

"If I am invited, I will, indeed. The viscount has not held the lease on Netherfield for very long. I wonder at him being so eager to entertain already."

Charlotte shrugged. "I do not know, but I suspect this is his way of repaying all the calls of the local gentlemen at one time." She handed a cup to Elizabeth. "It is the best way, really, and the most economical."

Elizabeth smirked as she lowered the cup from her mouth. "I cannot see a member of the peerage being concerned about economy overmuch."

Charlotte laughed. "Perhaps not, though given the state of things overall, it is possible."

"It is." Elizabeth conceded the point with a laugh. "I wonder if he will bring the invitations around himself, or send them in the post."

With that, the conversation turned to reminiscing about how things were done when Charlotte and Elizabeth were girls.

~~~***~~~

The very next day, Viscount Hucknall visited Longbourn. With him were Neville and Darcy, much to Elizabeth's delight. She knocked on her father's book room door, sticking her head around it with a grin when she heard the elderly man's command to enter.

"I heard there were visitors! You are not keeping them to yourself, are you, Papa?" Elizabeth's words were directed at her father, but her eyes devoured Darcy, who along with the other gentlemen, had risen when she entered.

"I would not think of it, Daughter." Bennet chuckled. "I was about to send them to you when you knocked."

"I do not mind visiting here, if you have no objections. I can have tea brought in, if you like?"

Neville was the first to respond. "I should enjoy visiting with the pair of you at the same time. Please allow it, Grandpapa."

Bennet's lips twisted into a wry grin. "You have always gotten your way with that look, young man." He shook his head with a sigh. "Very well. I was enjoying the gentlemen's company and we were discussing nothing a lady may not hear, so you can feel free to join us, Lizzy."

Chapter 6

"Thank you, Papa." Elizabeth flashed a quick grin before she stepped back into the hall to speak to the footman stationed there. As she entered again and made her way to her favored seat, she smiled at the gentlemen waiting. "I ordered tea and a light repast. Please do not feel obligated to eat; I happen to know my father ignored his breakfast tray today."

Bennet rolled his eyes, then tried to hide the grin that lifted his lips when the guests began to chuckle.

Darcy looked down at his hands, gripped together in his lap. His lips twitched as he listened to Elizabeth and her father banter together. He looked up at the sound of his name.

"Darcy is a crack shot, Grandpapa. I daresay he hit every bird he aimed at this morning; would you not say so, Frary?"

"I would," the viscount confirmed with a nod. "His skill is legendary in the family circle."

Darcy had begun to blush as the younger gentlemen praised him. He caught Elizabeth's eye and the admiration he saw there as she listened to his exploits made his chest puff out even as it made his face redder. "The pair of you did just as well. I was impressed with you both."

"I enjoyed hunting when I was a younger man." Bennet waved a hand in Neville's direction. "I taught my grandson all that he knows of sport. His father, good man that he is, does not enjoy such pursuits, so it fell to me to be the teacher."

"And a good one you were, Grandpapa."

Just then, the maid knocked on the door. Elizabeth rose to open it, leaving the gentlemen to speak more of their hunting exploits and expertise. She quietly directed the maid to set up the tea service on the table by the window and, once the girl had left, began to prepare the pot. Within a few minutes, she had begun pouring.

Darcy had watched as Elizabeth set about her task, and when it was clear she was ready to begin serving, he quickly rose to join her. "Shall I serve while you pour?"

Elizabeth was struck momentarily by the smile that brightened Darcy's countenance. She quickly gathered her wits, however, and thanked him for his thoughtfulness. "That would be wonderful.

Thank you." She handed him a cup and saucer. This is for my father. If you wait just a second, I will have a plate of sandwiches for him, as well."

Darcy nodded, holding the cup of tea while Elizabeth placed a couple small sandwiches on a plate. When she handed it to him, their fingers brushed. Darcy looked deep into her eyes, and the widening of the pupils assured him she felt the same pounding of the heart sensations he did. He longed to lean forward and kiss her, but a loud laugh from Bennet reminded him of their location. He drew back with a sigh, turning and delivering the cup and plate to the elderly gentleman.

Within a few minutes, Darcy and Elizabeth had served everyone their tea, and those who wished to eat had served themselves. Conversation flowed amongst the group in an easy rhythm. Suddenly, a knock sounded on the door and Elizabeth rose to answer it.

"Begging your pardon, ma'am. Mrs. Collins has come for a visit."

"Oh." Elizabeth paused, wiping the surprise from her face and replacing it with a smile. "Bring her in. We will require another tea service."

"Very good, ma'am." Mrs. Cowher dipped a curtsey before turning to hurry back to the entry hall.

Elizabeth shut the door and moved across the room again. "I apologize for interrupting. Mrs. Collins has come to visit. She should be here shortly."

Another knock and the door opened again. "Mrs. Collins, ma'am."

Charlotte stepped into the room, her head poking forward as though to peek to see who had preceded her. "I did not mean to intrude." Her gaze settled on Darcy and she smiled broadly.

"Not at all. Do come in." Elizabeth's lips lifted in a smile that did not reach her eyes. "We will just pull the chair over here from the table. Neville, you will do it for me, will you not?"

Elizabeth's nephew jumped at his aunt's words. He had stood, along with all the gentlemen except Mr. Bennet, when Charlotte entered the room. In short order, he had the chair positioned on the far side of his grandfather and the viscount. "How is this, Aunt Lizzy?"

"That will do. Thank you, Neville." Elizabeth turned to Charlotte. "Mrs. Cowher should be back shortly with a cup for tea. In the meantime, would you like some refreshments?"

Charlotte settled into her seat, her lips compressed. The corners lifted for a brief moment at her hostess' question. "That would be lovely. Thank you." She glanced at Darcy, then at the viscount and Mr. Bennet.

"My Lizzy tells me your nephews are back at school already." Elizabeth's father leaned back in his chair.

"Yes, they are. My brother and sister will be returning in another day or two, I should imagine." Charlotte glanced at Elizabeth as she accepted the plate of sandwiches and cakes. She smiled her thanks, then turned her attention back to Longbourn's master.

"I am sure they will be pleased to return. I was never one for travel, myself." Bennet sniffed, then leaned forward to poke at the cake Elizabeth had placed in front of him.

"Travel can be trying, I agree. Do you not think so, Mr. Darcy? You must travel quite a bit with homes in both Derbyshire and London." Charlotte smiled at Darcy.

Darcy looked away from Elizabeth, with whom he had been having a quiet side conversation, to reply. "Travel? Yes, long distances make for a tiring trip, and it seems more so now that I am older. The trains do make it better, thankfully."

"Yes, they do. My brother enjoys touring the places he goes now, since it is so much easier to get home than it used to be."

"John was slow to accept travel by rail, was he not?" Elizabeth tilted her head, watching her friend.

"He was. For a long time, he feared the train going off the rails, but time has proven his conjectures false and he has now accepted that they are safe, for the most part." Charlotte chuckled. "The first time he rode one, he came away with an entirely different feeling about it." Her eyes strayed to Darcy. "He could not get enough of it. Now he looks for trips to take that will allow him to ride in a train car."

Darcy smiled. "I think many of us do the same." He turned back to Elizabeth. "Have you traveled much, Miss Bennet?"

"I have, but not often. Mostly to London or to Kitty's home in Essex. I went to Newcastle to visit Lydia a few years ago, but I do not like to leave Papa for more than a day or two, so have not gone again." As she finished speaking,

Elizabeth saw just past Darcy's shoulder that the housekeeper was again entering. She smiled at him as she rose and murmured to excuse herself.

Darcy watched Elizabeth cross the room, his expression downcast. His attention was soon caught once again by Charlotte.

"Tell us about your estate, Mr. Darcy. I have heard much of its beauty from Neville."

Though he was always happy to speak of his Derbyshire home, Darcy wished it was Elizabeth he was speaking to. *I wonder what Mrs. Collins is about,* he thought. *Why would she try to draw my attention toward her so often? Is she flirting with me?* With an internal sigh, he forced his mind back to the topic at hand. "I am not certain I should be the one to describe it, for I cannot do so without bias. I love my home and find it the most beautiful in all England."

"I have heard the same. Is it true the house sits in a small valley, with wooded hills rising up behind it?" Charlotte's gaze was focused on Darcy, even as Elizabeth delivered a cup of tea into her hand.

For the remainder of the visit, the group listened to Charlotte's unending questions to Darcy and his increasingly reluctant replies. It was a relief a quarter hour later for the viscount to stand and remind the gentlemen of their additional appointments that day.

Chapter 7

To Darcy's frustration, he was unable to speak again to Elizabeth, beyond his farewell bow. He retained his stoic demeanor, climbing into the carriage behind his nephew.

As the equipage pulled away, the viscount turned to his uncle. "I say, that Mrs. Collins paid you particular attention, did she not?"

Darcy rolled his eyes. "She did, indeed."

Neville chuckled. "I would lay a pound she wants you for her next husband."

This time, Darcy shook his head but said nothing.

"She certainly appears to have set her cap at you." Hucknall smirked. "I have had the same experience; I recognize the behavior."

He nudged Darcy's boot with his foot. "What do you say?"

"What I say is that I am not interested. Not in Mrs. Collins, at any rate." Darcy sighed. "I do recognize her actions for what they are. It has been many years since I was chased so boldly but I have not forgotten. I simply did not expect it."

Hucknall examined Darcy closely. "Your interest lies elsewhere, it seems. I recall our conversation a few days ago at breakfast. I suppose I still may not tell Mother about it?"

Darcy glared at his nephew. "No, you may not. When there is something to tell her, I will do so."

"Well, I intend to host a ball soon and have asked her to be my hostess, so she will be able to see for herself." Hucknall examined his fingernails. "I will not have to say a word, for it is all in your looks."

Darcy grunted and turned toward the window, saying nothing. In the reflection of the glass, he could see his nephew nudge Neville and then the pair of them laughing. He rolled his eyes, then fell into contemplation of a pair of fine eyes in a pretty face.

~~~***~~~

A week later, Darcy stomped into Netherfield, fuming. He had been to Longbourn every day and every single visit with the lovely Elizabeth had been interrupted by her friend. Not only that, at every dinner and card party – and there had been an abundance of them – Charlotte Collins had inserted herself between him and the object of his affection. Darcy had long ago learned to treat others less meanly than he had been raised to do, but Mrs. Collins was enough to make him forget himself and fall back into old habits. *If only I was certain of Elizabeth's feelings.* Heaving a great sigh, he marched up the stairs to his chambers, intent on refreshing himself and changing his clothes.

An hour later, his ablutions completed and his temper somewhat regulated, Darcy joined his nephew in the billiards room.

"Good afternoon. How was your visit?" The viscount stood from where he had been bent over the table, lining up a shot.

Darcy rolled his eyes. "It was fine. Too short." He walked to the long case in the corner and chose a cue stick.

Hucknall stood his stick on end, his hands wrapped around it just under the tip. He tilted his head. "You were gone quite a while. What happened?"

Darcy's lips flattened. "Mrs. Collins happened."

The viscount winced. "I am sorry. I thought the reason you went to Longbourn so early was to avoid her."

"It was. However, Mrs. Collins seems to have somehow discovered that fact and came to see Miss Bennet on some pretext or other." Darcy gestured to the table, silently asking his nephew's permission to rack the balls for a new game.

Hucknall nodded. "How did Miss Bennet react?"

"She seemed a bit put out, to be honest. She is always gracious in her responses but I could swear I saw frustration and a bit of anger in her countenance, just for a brief second." Darcy shook the rack back and forth to tighten the balls, then lifted it.

"She welcomed her friend, though?" Hucknall leaned forward and placed the cue ball on the felt top of the table and shot it at the triangle of balls.

"She did. After that brief flash, no one would be able to guess her feelings were anything other than pleasant." Darcy noted to himself that Hucknall had sunk a solid-colored ball but kept talking. "She did her best to steer the conversation away from me and my interests, as well."

"Do you think Miss Bennet understands your distress at the situation?" Hucknall took another shot, cursing under his breath when his ball bounced off his uncle's and knocked it into a pocket.

Darcy grinned at his nephew's mistake. He took a position at the table and lined up a shot. "I do not know and I refuse to speculate. I was arrogant at one time in my life and would have assumed she was in love with me without worrying about the truth of the matter. I am not that person now. I would wish to know if my suit would be acceptable before I present it."

"I can understand that," Hucknall replied. He paused a moment but then added, "Mother will be here at the end of the week to organize the ball. Perhaps if you tell her about it, she will assist you in discovering Miss Bennet's feelings."

Darcy thrust his cue toward the white orb, knocking one of his striped ones into a pocket. He stood and moved, silent for a few moments as he figured out which shot to attempt this time. His decision finally made, he leaned over the table and spoke. "Perhaps." He shoved the stick, but this time it only glanced at the cue ball. He stood so the younger man could take his turn.

"If you did everything correctly, you could propose at the ball. Grand romantic gesture and all that." Hucknall glanced up from where he was bent over his stick.

Darcy rolled his eyes. "I am uncertain I am capable of romantic gestures." He waited while his nephew knocked a ball into a side pocket. "I will try, though. I confess I cannot imagine going back to Derbyshire without Miss Bennet."

"What about her father? She is his caretaker." Hucknall stood, having put another of his own balls into a pocket.

"If she and he were willing to move to Pemberley, I would be happy to have them both. If either of them wishes to stay in Hertfordshire for the remainder of his life, I am willing to do that, as well. As his son-in-law, I would be able to relieve some of the burden of running the place." Darcy shrugged. "It would be worth it to be husband to Elizabeth."

The viscount approached his uncle, laying his hand on the older gentleman's shoulder. "I am happy to hear you say this. If I were you, I would take the first opportunity to ask her opinion of it."

"I will do that. Thank you." Darcy nodded.

Without another word between them, the two continued on with their game.

~~~***~~~

Charlotte left Longbourn the next day, frustrated. Despite placing herself in front of Darcy every single day and at every event at which they were both in attendance, he exhibited no more interest in her now than he had the first day they had met. This was much easier with Collins, she thought to herself. On the heels of that recognition was the one that insisted her late husband had been much easier led in general than Mr. Darcy was.

Added to her dissatisfaction was that Charlotte knew time was running out to secure him. Viscount Hucknall had sent around invitations to a ball to be held in just four days. His mother, Countess Ashfield, had arrived three days ago to organize it. Charlotte had not met the lady, but rumor had it she was beautiful, gracious, and strong-willed. I do not know if I can sway her to favor me, and I do not have time to make the determination. What will I do?

Charlotte chewed her lip as she walked the path to her home. As she reached the turning, her brother was approaching from the other direction on his gelding.

"Ho, Charlotte!" His call pierced the quiet of the morning. "Wait for me and I will walk with you to the house."

Charlotte did as he requested, stepping back when the horse shifted. "Good morning, Brother. You are out and about early."

John Lucas lifted his brows. "I could say the same of you. I have noted you leaving the house much earlier lately."

Charlotte shrugged. "It will do me no good to deny it. I have been going to Longbourn to visit Eliza in the mornings."

Lucas' brows met just above his nose when he frowned. "Why so early?"

Charlotte looked around as they walked. With a sigh and a flattening of her lips, she admitted her reasons. "I discovered Mr. Darcy has been visiting before breakfast. I have been trying to persuade him to offer for me."

Lucas' brows rose again. "You have?" He was silent for a moment. "I suppose he is an eligible match."

"He is." Charlotte's tone was firm. "I would never have to worry about anything again. And, he is not ridiculous at all. It would be a pleasure to sit across from him at meals and converse with him before the fire in the evenings."

"He is very different from Collins, I grant you." Lucas looked at his sister out of the corner of his eye. "How has Darcy responded?"

Charlotte huffed. "He has not. He replies to my questions but never asks me any in return. There is no conversation between us but what I instigate." She rolled her eyes. "Frustrating man," she muttered.

"Would you like me to promote you to him? Perhaps hearing your praises sung by another will clear any confusion he might be feeling."

Charlotte thought about it for a long minute, but as the pair reached the steps to the house, she shook her head. Stopping, she laid her hand on her brother's arm. "No, do not. If he cannot see me for what I am by my own wiles, he will simply not see me at all. I will win him on my own or I will not."

Lucas hesitated, but then gave in to his sister's wishes. "Very well, I will remain silent, but Charlotte?" When he had her full attention, he continued. "I hope you are not pursuing Darcy because you fear being a burden to us here at Lucas Lodge. I know Father was not the best manager, but I have been able to grow our income and the value of the estate. I have diversified our holdings into factories and inventions. We have more than enough here for all of us. You are not a burden, and never could be. We love you, all of us, and wish you to remain with us forever." He squeezed her hand as he finished.

Charlotte gazed at her brother with tears in her eyes. "Thank you. I love all of you, as well. I promise you I will not allow myself to feel that I am an encumbrance to you."

With a smile, Lucas tucked his sister's hand under his elbow. Giving orders to the groom that appeared, he relinquished the gelding and escorted Charlotte into the house with a teasing comment.

Chapter 8

Later that morning, Darcy descended the stairs to break his fast with his sister. He entered the breakfast room to find her already seated and sipping hot tea.

"Good morning, Brother." Georgiana Frary lowered her cup to the table.

"Good morning, Your Grace." Darcy winked as he turned toward the sideboard, then chuckled to hear Georgiana's admonishment.

"That is 'My Lady' to you. I am not a duchess and you know it, you tease." The countess rolled her eyes behind her brother's back.

Darcy said nothing else. He could not, for he was attempting mightily to restrain his laughter. His plate finally full, he turned, lips twitching, and seated himself at his sister's right side. "Good morning, My Lady." Darcy laid his hand on Georgiana's and leaned to kiss her cheek. "You are looking quite lovely this morning."

"Thank you. You look very well yourself." The countess returned her brother's kiss before leaning back and looking at him critically. "You went riding?"

Darcy paused before he answered, his mouth full of kippers. He took the time to decide how to respond to Georgiana's inquiry. He swallowed. "I did." He hesitated a moment. "I also visited a neighbor."

Georgiana's right brow rose. "Oh?"

"Yes." Darcy dug into his eggs, not saying anything further.

With a stare that would stop most people in their tracks, the countess waited for her brother to say more, and when five long minutes had passed and she realized he did not intend to, she huffed. Narrowing her eyes at him, she pursed her lips and sniffed. "Oh, very well. Keep your own counsel for now. I will weasel it out of you sooner or later."

"You hope." Darcy winked and smirked.

Stiffly, Georgiana responded to his tease. "I am your closest relation. It is my right to know all of your affairs."

Darcy sat back, eyes wide. "You sound just like Lady Catherine when you do that."

Her own eyes widening, Georgiana clapped a hand over her mouth. "Oh, I did not mean to do

Zoe Burton

that. I am sorry. It just happens; I cannot control it."

The corners of Darcy's lips pulled down briefly. "I accept your apology." He shuddered. "Poor Ashfield, having to put up with that every day." He shook his head and applied himself to his breakfast once more.

Hucknall chose that moment to enter the breakfast room. "Good morning, Mother, Uncle."

"Good morning." Georgiana lifted her cheek for her son to kiss. She caressed his face. "You look very fine this morning. Has one of the local ladies caught your eye?"

Hucknall glanced at Darcy. "Oh, no, not mine. There is another whose eye has been well and truly caught, though."

"Indeed?" Georgiana had turned her attention back to her

plate and missed the look her son gave her brother. "Who would that be?"

"Oh, no one in particular." Hucknall cleared his throat. "I am afraid I am not at liberty to say."

Georgiana's brow twitched upwards as she lifted her head to stare at her son. "Which is it? No one, or someone you promised not to mention?"

Hucknall blushed a deep red. He stammered a response, throwing a desperate second glance at his uncle.

Seeing her son's eyes darting toward Darcy, the countess shifted her sharp-eyed stare in his direction.

Darcy studiously applied himself to his plate, not lifting his eyes. When he reached for his cup, he caught the intense gaze of his sister and his nephew's flustered appearance. "What?" He widened his eyes so as to appear as innocent as possible.

"Well, let us see." Georgiana leaned forward, wrists resting lightly on the edge of the table, knife and fork in her hands. "My son speaks of some mysterious person he is unable to name who has been bewitched by a local girl, you are suddenly and inordinately interested in the kippers and eggs before you, and you visited the neighbors at an unheard-of hour of the day."

Darcy's countenance was soon a similar shade as his nephew's. He cleared his throat. "What are you saying?"

Georgiana examined Darcy for a long time, staring into his eyes but saying nothing. Finally, she turned her attention back to her meal. "Nothing, Fitzwilliam." She finished breaking her fast before any of them spoke again. "I should like to visit some of the neighbors today. I wish for both of you to accompany me."

Darcy and Hucknall looked at each other before swiveling their gazes back to the countess.

"Of course."

"Yes, ma'am."

"Excellent." Georgiana rose, the gentlemen standing along with her. "I will be down in a half hour. Be ready." With that, she swept out the door.

Darcy and his nephew cleared their throats, looked at each other, and dropped into their chairs to finish eating.

~~~***~~~

Darcy spent the entire afternoon escorting his sister around to meet Netherfield's neighbors. He said not a word to her about Elizabeth. He did, however, determine to behave no differently than he usually did. If he were to be successful in his suit, Georgiana would discover his affection for the lady, regardless. He would not speak about it to her, but if she found out on her own, so be it.

Darcy had previous knowledge of where Elizabeth would be visiting today, so he took the lead in directing the driver from house to house. The third home they stopped at was Haye Park, where the Goulding family lived. As Darcy expected, the woman he was falling in love with was there.

Precedence required Georgiana, as the highest ranking

member of the party, be announced first, even though she was a stranger to the resident. Her son was quick to effect introductions after that, to the relief of the entire party. She was offered the best seat in the drawing room, one that she graciously accepted as she complimented Mrs. Goulding on the beauty of the decoration.

Darcy had identified Elizabeth's location immediately upon entering the room. At the earliest moment possible, he positioned himself upon the settee beside her as close as he dared.

"We meet again, Miss Bennet." Darcy's warm gaze roved Elizabeth's face, his eyes crinkling with his delighted smile.

"Indeed." Elizabeth laughed. "How are you this afternoon?"

"I am well." Darcy tilted his head toward Georgiana. "My sister insisted on making calls today, so here we are." He looked down for a moment, coloring slightly. "I confess, I made certain to direct us to this house at this particular time." He looked up through his lashes at Elizabeth, smiling at her grin.

"Very resourceful of you, sir." Elizabeth laughed and leaned closer to him. "I am pleased you did so," she whispered.

Darcy's heart stopped beating for a long moment. "Are you?" When Elizabeth nodded, the organ thumped and proceeded to beat loudly in his ears. "I am happy to hear it." He longed to pick up her hand and lace her fingers with his, but they were out in public and he had no desire to embarrass her.

On the other side of the room, Georgiana chatted with Mrs. Goulding and that lady's mother-in-law. Out of habit, her gaze swept the room, and she noted her brother's attention to Elizabeth. Making a mental note of it, she continued her conversation.

A few minutes passed, and the housekeeper entered to announce another guest. "Mrs. Collins, ma'am."

Georgiana smiled and nodded when the new visitor was introduced, then watched as the other woman greeted the rest of the party. She did not miss the way her brother and Elizabeth stiffened as Mrs. Collins approached them and sat on the other side of Darcy. She saw, though, that the trio was soon conversing, so she shrugged to herself.

On the other side of the room, Charlotte began to speak to Darcy, attempting to draw him into conversation.

"How are you today, Mr. Darcy? I did not expect to see you here." Charlotte smiled.

Darcy's lips lifted a little as he returned Charlotte's greeting. *I will not encourage her. Neither will I ignore Elizabeth. If not for the friendship between the two, I would cut Mrs. Collins and be done with it.*

A quarter hour later, Elizabeth rose and spoke to her hostess. "I should be going. It was so nice to see you today."

Georgiana popped out of her seat. "Look at the time! We should go, as well."

"Oh." Mrs. Goulding stood. "Time moves entirely too quickly when one is enjoying a visit, does it not? Thank you for coming, Lady Ashfield." She curtseyed. "You, as well, Miss Bennet. Please give your father our best."

Elizabeth smiled warmly. "I will do that." With a curtsey, she turned to make her way out of the room, finding Darcy behind her.

"May I escort you?" Darcy extended his arm to her.

"You may." Smiling, Elizabeth curled her hand around his forearm.

Darcy led Elizabeth out of the room. He leaned down and whispered, "Finally, we escape Mrs. Collins for a bit."

Elizabeth giggled, bringing her free hand over her mouth.

His eyes twinkling and a smirk twisting his lips, Darcy spoke quietly once more. "I should like to dance with you again."

Elizabeth looked up at him with her head tilted. "I should, as well."

"Do you plan to attend my nephew's ball?"

"I have not been invited."

Darcy reared back, eyes wide. He came to a complete stop a few feet from the line of carriages in front of the house. "How can that be?"

Elizabeth shrugged. "Perhaps the viscount intended to invite us personally?"

His lips pulled downward and his brow creased, Darcy hailed his nephew. "Hucknall." When the young man turned, Darcy gestured him closer.

"What is the matter?" The viscount's brow was wrinkled.

"How is it that Miss Bennet has not received an invitation to your ball?" Darcy glared at the younger man.

Hucknall's eyes grew wide. "She should have. I gave it to Dalrymple to give her. Something must have happened to prevent him."

"If you gave it to Neville, it is likely shoved into the pocket of his waistcoat, wrinkled beyond recognition." Elizabeth chuckled.

"You are probably right." The viscount shook his head. "I apologize. You and your father are definitely invited to the ball. Your sister and her family, as well. We will stop by their house and invite them on our way back to Netherfield."

"Thank you, sir. I would be happy to attend. My father may join me, but he usually stays at home."

Darcy laid his free hand over Elizabeth's and squeezed. "Since you are to attend, may I request your hand for the first set?"

Elizabeth softly smiled. "You may. I would be delighted to dance that set with you."

"Will you save me the supper set, as well?" Darcy's eyes roamed Elizabeth's face, his desire to kiss her nearly overwhelming.

"I will." Elizabeth's smile grew wider.

Darcy took a deep breath. "And ... the last? Will you dance the last with me?"

"And scandalize the neighborhood?" Elizabeth grinned. "I will."

"Dancing with you is worth any scandal that may occur." Darcy lifted Elizabeth's hand, kissing her fingers. He escorted her to her carriage, kissing her hand again before assisting her into the equipage. Once she was safely inside and the door shut, he instructed the coachman to move on and stood watching as the carriage trundled down the drive. Then, he hastened to his nephew's carriage, sitting on the rear-facing seat.

"So, Brother, tell me about Miss Bennet." Georgiana's eyes gleamed. "Then you can explain what in the world was going on with Mrs. Collins."

As the carriage made its way back to Netherfield, Darcy relieved his sister's curiosity, explaining his growing affection for Elizabeth Bennet and his frustration with Charlotte Collins' interference.

"That is a conundrum, is it not?" Georgiana flicked her gaze up and down over her brother's form before turning it toward the window. "Perhaps I can help?"

Darcy shrugged. "Perhaps, but I do not know how."

"Uncle, you told me the other day you were uncertain of Miss Bennet's regard."

"Surely not. Anyone with eyes can see that she is enamored of you, and you of her." Georgiana shook her head.

"She did give me an indication today that her feelings toward me are positive."

Georgiana snorted. "Call it that if you like, but I am telling you, she likes you very much." Shaking her head, she leaned back in her seat, muttering.

Darcy narrowed his eyes at his sister. "You know, superiority is very unattractive, especially in a woman."

Georgiana lifted her face to the ceiling. "I will not address that statement except to say Ashfield loves me despite it, so your theory is clearly flawed."

"Ashfield is stuck with you. He has no choice," Darcy replied, flatly.

Hucknall cleared his throat. "As fascinating as this glimpse into the interactions between siblings is, perhaps it might be better served if it waited until we were in the privacy of our home?" He looked between his mother and uncle. "If that is acceptable to both of you."

Georgiana looked down at her hands and Darcy blushed.

"You are correct. I apologize, to you, Nephew and to you, Sister."

"I am sorry, as well." Georgiana looked up. "I forgot myself."

Hucknall's stiff shoulders relaxed. "Good. Thank you both."

The trio rode in silence for a few minutes. It was Georgiana who broke it.

"I suspect Mrs. Collins has set her cap at you?"

Darcy's eyes moved away from the window to look at his sister. "It seems so."

"You, being a gentleman, have said nothing to her?"

"No, I have not." Darcy sighed. "I have no wish to be rude and she is Elizabeth's friend."

"Hmmm." Georgiana looked out the window but remained silent until the carriage slowed to make a turn. Then, she turned her gaze back to her brother. "Perhaps I can help you."

Darcy bit his lip and shrugged. "I do not know what you could do."

"I can give her a hint that you are not interested." Georgiana lifted her chin. "You have seen our aunts in action. Do you not think I am also capable of putting someone in their place?"

"Oh, I think you are eminently capable. I simply am uncertain how effective it would be for you to do so." Darcy glanced back out the window and then to his hands, which were clasped in his lap. He looked up at his sister once more and exhaled. "However, I give you leave to try. If it works, I will be forever grateful; if it does not." He shrugged again. "At least you made the attempt."

Georgiana smiled softly. "I will do my best."

Conversation moved on then to the ball, and soon, they were back at Netherfield.

Chapter 9

The day of the ball finally arrived. Georgiana had no opportunity to speak to Charlotte beforehand, but promised her brother she would say something when the lady went through the receiving line.

Darcy found he could not settle and was constantly pacing the floor or staring out a window, in part because of his sister interceding for him, and in part because he wanted this night to be perfect. He planned to propose to Elizabeth during the course of the evening and wished for nothing to distract from the beauty of the setting. He was almost relieved when he joined Georgiana to form the receiving line, despite his horror at being on display. He stood as still as possible, the fingers of one hand incessantly twisting the signet ring on the other. The arrival of the first guests distracted him slightly, but with every lull, the anxiety surged again.

Finally, she was there. Darcy looked away from the guest to whom he was speaking to see Elizabeth entering on the arm of her nephew. His heart stopped at the picture she made. She wore a gown of the deepest blue, split in the front, edged with lace, and displaying a bright white petticoat underneath. The lace-trimmed sleeves encircled her upper arms, leaving her shoulders bare. Darcy wished for nothing more than to run to her, wrap her in his arms, and make her his own. Only through the greatest exertion of his will was he able to refrain.

Within a few minutes, Elizabeth had made it down the receiving line. Darcy swallowed as she stood before him. He reached for her hand, and that feeling of coming home rushed over him, just as it did every time he touched her. He bowed, bringing her fingers to his lips to bestow a tender kiss on them. "Good evening, Miss Bennet."

Elizabeth's cheeks turned pink as her lips lifted in a teasing smile. "Good evening, Mr. Darcy. I eagerly await our dances."

Darcy squeezed the fingers he had yet to release. "I do, as well." The sound of his sister's throat clearing shook him out of his dazed condition. He let go, feeling bereft, and bowed again.

"I will be waiting." Elizabeth curtseyed a second time and drifted away, her gaze lingering on Darcy's tall form.

At the other end of the line, Georgiana had witnessed the interaction between Darcy and Elizabeth. She nodded to herself, turning her attention back to her son and the next set of guests. She lost count of the number of people she spoke to, but heard the musicians tuning up and knew the last of the guests would soon be walking through the door. Where is Mrs. Collins? I surely did not miss her! Suddenly, there Charlotte was, entering the house behind her brother and sister-in-law.

When her turn came to greet the viscount and his family, Charlotte curtseyed. "Good evening, Lord Hucknall, Lady Ashfield, Lord Ashfield."

The gentlemen greeted Charlotte, then Georgiana spoke. "Good evening, Mrs. Collins. I am so happy you could attend. I have invited a couple single gentlemen who are friends of my husband's. They have lost their wives and are making their first forays into society after their mourning. I would take it as a personal favor if you agreed to dance with them."

"Oh!" Charlotte's eyes widened and she shot a glance down the line toward Darcy before giving her attention back to Georgiana. "I would be happy to."

"Excellent! I will be sure to seek you out later, to introduce them to you." Georgiana smiled warmly. She looked toward the ballroom. "Oh, there is Miss Bennet! Have you seen her gown?" When Charlotte declared she had, Georgiana continued. "Is it not absolutely stunning? I have not seen a gown quite that beautiful. I told her when she arrived that I must have a pattern for it to give my modiste. I should like to make the earl look at me the way my brother looked at Miss Bennet." She leaned in toward Charlotte. "You must work to keep gentlemen interested even after the wedding, as I am certain you can attest." She leaned back again and sighed. "Darcy could hardly take his eyes off her when they spoke. I confess; the family has great hopes of a match being made there. Miss Bennet is such an elegant lady, and she fits in so well with us." Suddenly, the music transitioned from unorganized squawking to a smooth melody. "Oh! I am to open the dancing with my son. Please, do excuse me. As soon as I can, I will find you!" With that, Georgiana took Hucknall's hand and pulled him away.

Charlotte flashed a half-hearted smile at her hostess as the other woman left her behind. Darcy had already fled the area, and she could see him stride toward Elizabeth. She sighed. Wandering into the ballroom, she took her customary place with the matrons. Once she had greeted the other ladies, she lost herself in thoughts of Darcy and her plans that rapidly seemed to be coming to naught. Georgiana's words echoed in her mind. Darcy could hardly take his eyes off her when they spoke. I confess; the family has great hopes of a match being made there. Miss Bennet is such an elegant lady, and she fits in so well with us. "Well, Lizzy Bennet," Charlotte murmured, "we shall see about that. One gentleman is much like the rest. I was able to draw Collins to my side; Darcy cannot be all that difficult. Until the vows are spoken, he is available."

Charlotte sat out the first two sets, watching as Darcy danced with Elizabeth and then his sister. She rose and edged through the crush of people to the side of the room where punch was set out on a long table. She accepted a cup from a footman, smiling her thanks, and meandered that side of the room, slowly making her way toward the countess and Darcy. She stopped near the spot where they were dancing, in the hopes of receiving a request for a set.

The music stopped and the dancers applauded, smiling at each other and laughing. Charlotte watched as Darcy said something to his sister, holding his arm out toward Georgiana. Suddenly, Charlotte became aware of Elizabeth standing beside her.

"Hello, Charlotte. I was looking for you." Elizabeth smiled.

"There are so many people, I was not certain I would find you." She laughed.

Charlotte smiled, a strained lift of the corners of her lips. "It is crowded." She glanced around. "The viscount must have invited half of London, as well as the four and twenty families in the area."

"I suspect you are right."

Darcy and Georgiana had reached them, and the eyes of both ladies were riveted upon Darcy's handsome mien.

"You dance divinely together." Charlotte's smile this time appeared more sincere. "You are both so graceful."

"Thank you." Georgiana's lips twitched, as though she was fighting a grin. "I forced my brother to practice with me last night. My husband, as well." She looked around. "Oh, there he is! I promised him this set."

A tall, blond gentleman with regal bearing stepped to Georgiana's side. "There you are, my dear." He took hold of her hand and tucked it between his elbow and his side. "Darcy, if you are finished with my wife for now, I should like to borrow her. I would rather not waste all that practice last night." Lord Ashfield winked at his brother-in-law.

Darcy laughed. "Oh, yes, she is yours the rest of the evening, if you really want her."

Georgiana glared at her brother. "I am not so certain I like how that sounds."

Ashfield patted his wife's hand. "All is well, dear. I am enamored enough of you that it will not matter if your brother wants you."

Georgiana sniffed and her frown at her brother changed to an adoring look into her husband's eyes. "I am so happy about that, too."

Darcy groaned. "Off with you both before we are all sickened by the sweetness."

Elizabeth and Charlotte both giggled as the couple took Darcy's words to heart and wandered away.

Darcy looked at the ladies before him. He noticed Elizabeth tilting her head at her friend with a raised eyebrow and knew it was a hint to him to ask her to dance. As much as he both disliked the exercise in general and wished to avoid Charlotte in particular, he found he could deny Elizabeth nothing.

"Would you honor me with your hand for the next set, Mrs. Collins?"

Charlotte smiled widely. "Of course I would! Thank you for asking."

The musicians began to play once more and Charlotte turned to Elizabeth, shoving her cup at her. "Please, do take this for me. Thank you so much." She turned and latched onto Darcy's arm.

Darcy cleared his throat. He bowed his head to Elizabeth. "Until later, Miss Bennet."

Elizabeth lifted her wide stare from the cup she suddenly found herself holding to Darcy and her friend. "Until later." She lifted the corners of her lips briefly. When the gentleman she had fallen in love with and her friend turned toward the dance floor, she mentally shook herself, searching for a footman to take the cup.

Charlotte clasped her hands together, her heart racing. This is my chance, she thought. I have a single opportunity to get what I want. Do not mess this up, Charlotte Collins! When she heard the dance called out, she grinned. The steps of a jig were lively, and it was often difficult to keep up.

The first few minutes went well. Charlotte and Darcy held hands and hopped down the line as the dance required. It was when they had to swing each other around that disaster – or in this case Charlotte – struck.

Just as Darcy let go of Charlotte's hands, she appeared to stumble. She grabbed his sleeve with one hand as she fell to the floor, ripping it nearly off at the shoulder. A cry burst from her throat as she landed awkwardly on the opposite arm.

Darcy tripped over Charlotte's skirts and legs, and to onlookers it seemed as though he would fall right on top of her. However, his frequent participation in the art of fencing had kept him nimble, and he was able to keep himself upright. The dancers on either side of the unfortunate couple stopped, their progress impeded by the accident.

Darcy's inelegant careening came to a stop a foot or so the other side of his dance partner. He turned immediately and offered her his hand. "Are you well, Mrs. Collins? May I help you rise?"

Charlotte frowned, cradling her injured limb with her good hand. How did he not fall? "Yes, please." She accepted his hand, but instead of using her legs to assist Darcy in helping her to stand, she forced him to lift her with all his strength. This resulted in another stumble. Though he nearly went down, he pulled back and managed to raise her to her feet.

Charlotte huffed as she again brought her rapidly swelling arm to her chest. She could hear the couples nearby talking about the incident and speculating that she had tried to compromise Darcy. She began to blush.

"*Are* you well? Perhaps we should sit out the remainder of the set so you can rest and recover?" Darcy peered into Charlotte's face, seeing the pain in her expression.

"Yes, I would like that. Thank you." Charlotte spoke through gritted teeth.

A few short minutes later, Darcy had led Charlotte to the

side of the room and seated her in a chair. Elizabeth rushed to them.

"Oh, Charlotte, I saw you fall! Are you well? Can I get you anything? Some punch, or maybe something stronger?" Elizabeth picked up her friend's hand and chafed it.

"I am well, yes. I would imagine I will have a nice bruise in the morning." Charlotte attempted to smile, but her disappointment, anger and pain made it appear more as a grimace.

"You are holding your arm; did you fall on it?" Elizabeth frowned as she noticed the wince her friend made.

Charlotte looked up as her brother suddenly loomed at her side.

"Are you well, Sister?" At Charlotte's nod, John Lucas'

hands landed on his hips. "What was that all about? Do you hear what people are saying? I have never been more embarrassed in my life, not even when Father nattered on about his knighthood." He turned to Darcy. "I am sorry, sir, that your coat was damaged. I will pay for repairs, or for a new coat, whichever you think is best."

Darcy looked at one arm and then the other. "I had not been aware that it ripped until just now." He lifted the material up to his shoulder. "Do not be concerned. It appears to be a simple repair; the garment is not ruined. My valet will have it right as rain in no time, I am certain." He looked up. "I am more concerned with Mrs. Collins' health, but she assures us she is well."

Lucas nodded once, then turned to examine his sister from

149

head to toe, focusing his gaze on the arm she cradled. "It does look as though you have injured yourself. I believe the apothecary is in attendance." He looked around, found a footman, gestured the servant to come closer, and then instructed him to find the local medical expert.

Charlotte rolled her eyes. She clamped her lips shut.

"Unless you require my assistance, I will go up and change my coat." Darcy looked from sister to brother and when he received their assurances that he was not needed, he offered his elbow to Elizabeth and led her away. "You will wait for me to return?"

"I will." Elizabeth looked up at him from the corner of her eye. "After all, the next set is the supper set and that is promised to you. I would hate to miss it."

Darcy grinned. "True." He stopped their forward progress when he reached the staircase. He looked up, longing to be able to ask Elizabeth to accompany him to his chambers while he repaired his appearance. He swallowed that desire down and instead, took her hands in his. "I will return in just a few minutes. Do not move."

Elizabeth's eyes twinkled up at Darcy. "I will be here, as long as you hurry."

Darcy kissed her hands, then stepped back. "Stay."

"Run!" Elizabeth waved her hand at the steps.

With a grin, Darcy did as his beloved bid him. Five minutes later, he returned wearing a different coat. "We are in luck. My valet had inadvertently packed two of my best suits. No one will be the wiser that this is not the coat I began the evening with."

"Unless they watched your dance with Charlotte." Elizabeth smirked.

Darcy rolled his eyes. "Right." He paused, tilting his head and listening to the applause and the music, which immediately started up again for the second dance of the set. "Shall we take a stroll?" He could feel the ring in his pocket as it rubbed against his watch. His plan had been to wait for supper to propose, but Charlotte's fall and this sudden opportunity to get Elizabeth alone had opened up the possibility of fulfilling his desire now.

"I would like that." Elizabeth took the arm he proffered and allowed him to lead her down the hall. "Where are we going?"

"I thought we might get some fresh air on the balcony."

"I like that. It would not be a ball if I did not visit the outdoors in my gown for a few minutes." Elizabeth grinned at Darcy's chuckle.

"You often visit dark balconies in a ballgown, then?"

Elizabeth shrugged. "The moon is almost always full when balls are held and the weather is often very fine. I prefer the out of doors above just about anything, so yes, I do often visit dark balconies in a ballgown. Always alone, though."

Darcy led Elizabeth through a back entrance to the ballroom and across to the outside doors. He said nothing about her last statement, but the possessive inner man that had taken root as he had fallen in love jumped in glee, because it meant she had probably never been kissed before.

The couple stepped outside to find the wide space empty. Darcy drew Elizabeth to the side, where some large plants in pots had been placed and would provide privacy, in case other couples decided to make use of the space before Darcy was finished. He turned, facing Elizabeth, taking her hands, and looking down into her upturned face.

"I have never met anyone like you before." Darcy's soft words floated on the air between him and Elizabeth. "You are kind and warm, and something else, something I cannot identify." He stared into her eyes and took a deep breath. "I have fallen in love with you, and I am fairly certain you return my sentiments. I feel as though I have come home when I am in your presence and I cannot begin to imagine leaving here without you.

"I know that you are your father's caretaker, and I am willing to do whatever you wish as far as he is concerned." Darcy paused again. "What I am trying to say is, I want to make you mine, forever. I never wish to be parted again. Will you marry me?"

Elizabeth's eyes filled with tears. She blinked, and one rolled out of each eye and down her cheeks as a bright smile lit her face. "Thank you for your offer. I happily accept. I love you, too."

"Elizabeth." Darcy wrapped his arms around her, pulling her into his embrace. "I love you so very much." His lips found hers, drawing them both into a swirling morass of feeling. Noise spilling from the ballroom when another couple stepped outside called them both back to the present and their position. They separated just a bit, looking at each other and smiling.

"Thank you, my love," Darcy whispered. "You have made me the happiest of men."

Elizabeth caressed Darcy's cheek. "It is only fair, for you have made me the happiest of women."

Darcy leaned his head into Elizabeth's touch, but when voices began to intrude on their solitude, he pulled away. Grabbing her hand, he encouraged her to go in. "They will be serving supper soon. We must share our news with our families." He paused at the door, kissing Elizabeth's fingers before opening the portal and pulling her through.

Epilogue

Ten days later, Darcy and Elizabeth married in Longbourn Church. They had thought to have the ceremony after Christmas, but Mr. Bennet had insisted it be soon.

"There is no need for you to have a long engagement. Purchase a common license and marry next week."

"Papa! What would people think?"

"Hang what people will think!" Bennet waved his hand to emphasize his point. When his daughter gasped at his language, he continued. "One of the benefits of reaching the ripe old age of eighty is that I can say whatever I wish with no fear of censure. I am serious. I am living on borrowed time and wish to see you settled before I shuffle off this mortal coil."

Darcy interrupted the argument. "I will travel to town and obtain a special license. My uncle is the archbishop; he is getting ready to retire, but I am certain he will happily grant me one."

Elizabeth immediately protested. "The expense! We do not need a special license; a common one is well enough."

"We can afford it, and it will be no hardship, other than being away from you for a se'ennight." Darcy lifted Elizabeth's hand, which he had been holding, and kissed her fingers.

Elizabeth stared at Darcy for a few moments, trying to read his expression. Finally, she gave in. "Very well. If you wish it, you may go get one."

Darcy grinned at her. "Thank you." He kissed her hand again.

Now, here they were. Darcy stood at the front of the church, his brother-in-law at his side. He knew he should be nervous, but he was not. In a few minutes, he would marry the woman of his dreams. He had her heart and she had his, and they would be joined forever. He was eager to get on with it.

When the guests had all settled in, the organist began to play. All eyes turned to the back of the church, Darcy's included. When he saw Elizabeth, everyone else faded. He did not see her father in his wheeled chair being pushed by Neville. He did not hear the murmurs of the guests remarking on how well the bride looked. There was only Elizabeth and her twinkling eyes and eager smile.

Two hours later, the vows spoken and a bit of wedding cake consumed, Darcy and Elizabeth departed in his traveling coach for a few days of honeymooning at a nearby leased estate.

~~~***~~~

Mr. Bennet lived long enough for his favorite daughter to return from her wedding trip. Seeing Elizabeth so happy fulfilled his last wish, and he passed quietly in his sleep.

Though she spent the first year of her marriage in mourning, Elizabeth knew her father had died happy. She was at peace, married to the best man she knew.

The End

Before you go …

If you enjoyed this book, please consider leaving a review at the store where you purchased it.

Also, consider joining my mailing list at https://mailchi.mp/ee42ccbc6409/zoeburtonsignup.

~Zoe

About the Author

Zoe Burton first fell in love with Jane Austen's books in 2010, after seeing the 2005 version of Pride and Prejudice on television. While making her purchases of Miss Austen's novels, she discovered Jane Austen Fan Fiction; soon after that she found websites full of JAFF. Her life has never been the same. She began writing her own stories when she ran out of new ones to read.

Zoe lives in a 100-plus-year-old house in the snow-belt of Ohio with her Boxer, Jasper. She is a former Special Education Teacher, and has a passion for romance in general, *Pride and Prejudice* in particular, and NASCAR.

Zoe belongs to the Jane Austen Society of North America, and JASNA's Ohio North Coast chapter.

Connect with Zoe Burton

Email:
zoe@zoeburton.com

Facebook:
https://www.facebook.com/ZoeBurtonBooks

https://www.facebook.com/groups/BurtonsBabes/

Pinterest:
https://www.pinterest.com/zoeburtonauthor/

Instagram:
https://www.instagram.com/zoeburtonauthor/

Website:
https://zoeburton.com

Join my mailing list:
https://mailchi.mp/ee42ccbc
6409/zoeburtonsignup

Support me at Patreon:
https://www.patreon.com/zo
eburtonauthor

Me at Austen Authors:
http://austenauthors.net/zoe
-burton/

More by Zoe Burton

Regency Single Titles:

I Promise To...

Lilacs & Lavender

Promises Kept

Bits of Ribbon and Lace (Short Stories-available exclusively to newsletter subscribers)

Decisions and Consequences

Mr. Darcy's Love

Darcy's Deal

The Essence of Love

Matches Made at Netherfield

Darcy's Perfect Present

Darcy's Surprise Betrothal

To Save Elizabeth

Darcy Overhears

Merry Christmas, Mr. Darcy!

Darcy's Secret Marriage

Darcy's Christmas Compromise

Darcy's Predicament

Darcy's Uneasy Betrothal

Westerns:

Darcy's Bodie Mine

Bundles:

Darcy's Adventures

Forced to Wed

Promises

Mr. Darcy Finds Love (available exclusively to newsletter subscribers)

The Darcy Marriage Series Books 1-3

Mr. Darcy, My Hero

Coming Together

The Darcy Marriage Series:

Darcy's Wife Search

Lady Catherine Impedes

Caroline's Censure

Contemporary Settings:

Darcy's Race to Love

Georgie's Redemption

Darcy's Caution

www.ingramcontent.com/pod-product-compliance
Lightning Source LLC
Chambersburg PA
CBHW030343180626
46812CB00007B/2733